The Red 1

The Red Notebook

Benjamin Constant

Translated by Douglas Parmée

ALMA CLASSICS

ALMA CLASSICS LTD
London House
243-253 Lower Mortlake Road
Richmond
Surrey TW9 2LL
United Kingdom
www.almaclassics.com

The Red Notebook first published in French as Le Cahier rouge in 1907
This translation first published by Alma Classics Ltd in 2011
Translation and Introduction © Douglas Parmée, 2011
Cover image © Corbis Images

Printed and bound by CPI Group (UK) Ltd, Croydon, CR0 4YY

ISBN: 978-1-84749-276-0

Contents

Introduction

As an author of autobiographical fiction, Henri-Benjamin Constant de Rebecque is best known for his novel *Adolphe*, which, first published in 1816, has enjoyed continuing success. In later life he was to write many works on politics and religion, but he also wrote two shorter autobiographical works, which remained long unpublished: *The Red Notebook* (named after the cahier in which the text was written), which first appeared in 1907, and part of an unfinished novel, *Cécile*, which carries his autobiography on from *The Red Notebook* and did not appear in print until 1951.

Given its brevity, relative unfamiliarity and rather fragmentary structure, *The Red Notebook* has never achieved the stature of *Adolphe*, although a number of the incidents it relates also appear in that novel. It is, or purports to be, an autobiography covering the period from the author's birth in 1767 to his twentieth year. Internal evidence and Constant's correspondence suggest that its composition was spread over many years; the author may have started work on it as early as the mid-1790s and did not set it finally aside until well after the publication of *Adolphe* in 1816. Its readers will benefit from this lengthy period of gestation: the delay gave Constant time to manipulate facts, leave many out, and, above all, express or hint at the views of a mature man in his younger self. But just as readers of *Adolphe* are not concerned about the exact blend of truth and fiction, we can read *The Red Notebook* as a fictional *Bildungsroman*, a portrait of a young man growing up – a process by no means complete by the end of the text. (Indeed, the author's diaries suggest that he himself never truly grew up.) The narrator of *The Red Notebook* is by no means the only protagonist in fiction of whom this might be said: Stendhal's Fabrice in *The Charterhouse of Parma* and Julien Sorel in *The Red and the Black* immediately come to mind.

The Red Notebook teems with odd characters and odd events, so many, indeed, that one of its messages seems to be that so-called "normal" people are rather rare birds. After the narrator the most significant figure in *The Red Notebook* is the former's father, who frequently emerges from the background with important consequences. Constant's father was the colonel of a Swiss regiment in the service of Holland – it was a common practice for Swiss regiments to act as mercenaries for other nations. It is, moreover, important to note the significance of Benjamin Constant's Swiss origins: Switzerland was a neutral country and in those troubled times its citizens could travel far more freely in Europe than those from countries often at war. Constant's father as represented in the book is an enigma: well intentioned, kindly and, for reasons never fully disclosed – ambiguity is also one of Constant's constant ploys – apparently an excessively, almost incredibly indulgent parent. He is also muddle-headed, prejudiced and incompetent – in real life he caused members of his regiment to mutiny, which led to a court martial and his dismissal from the service, an incident referred to in *The Red Notebook*, with little detail, as an act of "injustice".

These first twenty years of Constant's life as related in the book fall into a number of sections; it is, in part, a picaresque novel, containing much travel – being constantly on the move becomes a way of life for Benjamin. And we see a good deal of the other main feature of the picaresque novel: roguery. It also includes a number of other strands, notably a hint of Constant's later, naturally very complicated political commitments, but the tale itself ends inconclusively with a trivial, amusing anecdote – does this inconclusiveness itself not form a part of its moral? We are left with the impression of an interesting young man: intelligent, gifted, sensitive – as well as snobbish, selfish, vulnerable, immature and quite unready to come to terms with life. Written as it was by the older Constant, it contains cold-blooded assessments of the author's early weaknesses, vanity and self-deceit; but readers will find themselves wondering whether he might not have known that he was behaving like a clown even at the time – on this matter we are left constantly in suspense.

The story of Constant's life is taken up in *Cécile*, which covers the period from 1793 to 1808. Constant had already written of his desire to settle down, of his need for affection, and indeed one of his first priorities as described in this later book is to get married, although this turns out to be complete folly. He later said (he was an expert in hindsight) that he married out of pity, weakness and a desire to make a personal commitment – as well, perhaps, as masochism: his cousin Rosalie describes his wife as ugly, deeply pockmarked, with bloodshot eyes, and very skinny. How odd! Even more odd is that, quite soon, despite her appearance, she finds a man who loves her. After the end of the author's marriage *Cécile* goes on to recount his further sentimental education until, finally, the literary intellectual Madame de Staël arrives on the scene and, after further typical hesitations, Constant realizes that he has found his true love, or rather his true theme. He dropped *Cécile*, never to return to it, and started on his masterpiece, *Adolphe*.

He continued to work on *The Red Notebook*, but the publication of *Adolphe* marked the end of Constant's interest in publishing fiction. He turned to politics, an interest he pursued for the rest of his life and on which he wrote prolifically. He also wrote and published a great deal on religion: his history of polytheism (briefly, amusingly and slightingly mentioned in *The Red Notebook*) appeared posthumously in 1833.

The Red Notebook is an ingenious and incontrovertibly amusing piece of writing which, despite lacking an ending, can bear comparison with any short fiction, even with the stories of such a master as Mérimée. It covers a wide range of experiences, some of them absurd, which surely makes Constant somewhat of a precursor of modern trends. Certain sections are almost farcical – some of his extravagant love affairs, for example – but they are recounted with a deadpan factuality that makes them credible. His discovery of his "real self" in England, even if it is in part untrue, gives charming insights into youthful, quickly discarded enthusiasms as well as into others permanently valid: his discovery of natural beauty is an obvious example, as is his urge to travel, something that has become endemic. One of the principal charms of *The Red Notebook* is Constant's consistent volatility and uncertainty: nothing is quite what it seems for very long, the tone is often ironic and much remains ambiguous, attributes very appealing to modern sensibilities. To this extent Constant's work is very up to date, as well as having the attractively piquant flavour of the eighteenth century.

Flaubert once stated, doubtless in one of his black moods, that children read for diversion, that it is the ambitious who read to be instructed and that the best reason for reading is in order to learn how to live. If we apply these rather magisterial statements to *The Red Notebook*, we must admit that we gain very little hard knowledge from the work: an interesting glimpse into travel in England and into English country life in general, perhaps, as well as a picture of life in Paris, albeit in certain, rather limited, circles; but it doesn't add up to much. Nevertheless, the very essence of *The Red Notebook,* the leaven of the whole lump, is its teaching about life and how it should be lived – indeed, warnings of how *not* to live are scattered in abundance throughout the work – as we get to know very intimately a narrator who is just beginning to learn this difficult art.

– Douglas Parmée

I am glad to acknowledge my debt to the edition of *The Red Notebook* published in 1991 by the Cambridge Daemon Press, edited by C.P. Courtney. Dr Courtney has forgotten more about Constant's work than most people have ever known; his edition has proved invaluable.

The *Chronologie* of the Pléiade edition of a selection of Constant's works, first published in 1957, gives an excellent idea of Constant's restlessness.

The Red Notebook

I WAS BORN IN LAUSANNE on 25th October 1767. My mother, Henriette de Chandieu, came from an old French family which had taken refuge in the Swiss canton of Vaud to avoid religious troubles; my father was Juste Constant de Rebecque, a colonel in a Swiss regiment in the service of Holland. My mother died a few days after I was born.

1772

The first tutor whom I can remember more or less distinctly was a German. He used to beat me a lot and then hug me so that I wouldn't complain to my father. I promised not to and faithfully kept my word, but when, despite that, it was discovered, my father dismissed him. He had, incidentally, worked out a very ingenious method of teaching me Greek: he had suggested to me that we should have a private language, just for the two of us, that only we should know. I enthusiastically agreed. First of all, he invented an alphabet made up of Greek characters, then we started to make a dictionary in which every French word was translated by a Greek one. All this became superbly imprinted in my mind because I thought it was I who was doing the inventing, and I already knew a whole lot of Greek words and was

3

starting to give these words, which had been created by me, some general laws, which means that, when my tutor was dismissed, I was learning Greek grammar. I was at the time five years old.

1774–76

When I was seven, my father took me with him to Brussels and wanted to take over my education himself. He soon gave up and got me a French tutor, Monsieur de la Grange, chief surgeon in his regiment. Monsieur de la Grange was a professed atheist. Apart from that, as far as I can remember, he was also rather second-rate, very ignorant and extremely vain. He tried to seduce the daughter of the music master who was teaching me piano. He had a number of scandalous affairs. Finally he took me with him to share rooms in a house of ill fame, where it was easier for him to indulge in his pleasures. My father arrived from his regiment in a fury and Monsieur de la Grange was sacked.

While I was waiting to be given another mentor, my father sent me to live with my music teacher and I spent a few months with him. This family, which had been lifted by the musical talents of their father from a very lowly social position, fed me and looked after me very well but could do nothing for my education. I was given a few teachers whose lessons I skipped and there was a library nearby which contained every novel which had ever been written and all the anti-religious works fashionable at the time. For eight to ten hours a day I read everything I could lay my hands on, from La Mettrie to Crébillon's novels. My head and my eyes have felt the effects ever since.

1776–77

From time to time I was visited by my father; he had met an ex-Jesuit who had suggested himself as being suitable to take charge of me but nothing came of it, I don't know why. At about the same time, a former French lawyer, who'd had to leave the country as a result of some shady business and was living in Brussels with a young tart whom he was passing off as his housekeeper, wanted to set up a teaching establishment and offered his services so persuasively that my father thought he'd found the right man. Monsieur Gobert agreed, for a very high fee, to take me into his house. He only gave me lessons in Latin – a language which he knew very poorly – and history, which he was teaching me for the sole purpose of getting me to copy out a book he had written on the subject and wanted additional copies of. But my handwriting was so poor and I was so careless that I had to keep on starting every copy over and over again. After working on it for more than a year, I never managed to get beyond the introduction.

1777–78

Meanwhile, Monsieur Gobert and his mistress had become the talk of the town and my father came to hear of it. There followed scenes which I myself witnessed and I left my third tutor's house convinced for the third time that these men who'd been given the task of tutoring me and forming my character were themselves very ignorant and very immoral.

My father took me back with him to Switzerland, where I spent some time on his country estate, under his charge alone. One of his friends told him about a quite elderly Frenchman who was living in retirement in La Chaux-de-Fonds, near Neuchâtel, and who had the reputation of being intelligent and knowledgeable. My father made enquiries and learnt that Monsieur Duplessis – that was his name – was an unfrocked monk who had escaped from his monastery, changed his religion and was living in reclusion in order not to be pursued by the French, even in Switzerland.

Although this information was hardly very encouraging, my father sent for Monsieur Duplessis, who turned out to be better than his reputation. So he became my fourth tutor. He was a man of very weak character, but kind and witty. My father immediately conceived a great contempt for him and didn't hide his feelings from me – hardly a good preparation for the relationship between teacher and pupil. Monsieur Duplessis performed his duties to the best of his ability and I made a great deal of progress. I spent just over a year with him, in Switzerland as well as in Brussels and Holland. At the end of that time, my father became fed up with him and made plans for me to go to a university in England.

1778–79

Monsieur Duplessis left to become tutor to a young Comte d'Aumale. Unfortunately, this young man had a quite good-looking sister, very loose in her behaviour, who thought it would be fun to turn the poor monk's head. He fell passionately in love with her, though he hid the fact because his position in the household, his fifty years of age and his looks offered little hope of success. Then he discovered that a wig-maker, not so old and not so ugly, had been more successful. He started to do all sorts of wild things for which he was shown no mercy. He went out of his mind and ended up blowing his brains out.

1779–80

Meanwhile, my father took me with him to England and after a very short stay in London went with me to Oxford. He soon realized that that university, where the English go to finish their studies at the age of twenty, wouldn't be suitable for a boy of thirteen. So he confined himself to teaching me English, going on a few excursions around Oxford for his own pleasure, and we left after two months with a young Englishman who'd been recommended to him as being a suitable teacher for me, despite not having any title or claim to be a tutor, something which my father had grown to loathe after the four previous experiences. Hardly had we set off with Mr May before my father began to find him ridiculous and unbearable. He confided his impressions to me, as a result of which I treated my new companion with constant ridicule and disrespect from then on.

Mr May spent a year and a half in our company in Switzerland and Holland. We lived for quite a while in the little town of Geetruidenberg. It was there that I fell in love for the first time. She was the daughter of the Governor, an old officer and friend of my father. I'd spend every day writing her long letters, none of which I ever sent, and I left without having declared my passionate love to her, which lasted for a good two months.

1780–81

I've met her since and the thought that I'd loved her aroused in her an interest or perhaps just curiosity to learn things about me. Once she made a sort of move to ask me about what my feelings had been for her but we were interrupted. Some while later, she got married and died in childbirth. My father, whose only desire was to get rid of Mr May, seized the first opportunity to send him back to England.

1781–82

So we went back to Switzerland where he turned to a Monsieur Bridel to give me a few lessons; he was quite well-educated but very pedantic and very pompous. My father didn't take long to feel shocked by the self-importance, the disrespectful tone and the ill manners of this latest mentor he'd chosen for me and, exasperated by all his failed attempts to provide me with a private education, decided to find me, a fourteen-year-old, a place in a German university.

The Margrave of Anspach who was in Switzerland at the time, suggested Erlangen. My father took me there and himself presented me to the little court of the Dowager Margravine of Bayreuth, which was her residence. She welcomed us with the eagerness that all bored princes or princesses feel for anyone who comes from across the border to amuse them. The Margravine took to me; in fact, as I would say the first thing that came into my head, poked fun at all and sundry and expressed, quite wittily, the most ludicrous ideas. I must have been quite an amusing person to meet, for a German court. For his part, the Margrave treated me equally kindly, giving me a title as Groom of the Bedchamber at his court, where I used to go and play faro and run up gambling debts which my father made the mistake of being kind enough to pay.

1783

During my first year at university I studied a great deal but, at the same time, did a lot of very silly things. The old Margravine forgave me for all my stupidities and liked me all the more, and, in such a small town, the favour that I was enjoying at court compelled all those who judged me more severely to keep their opinions to themselves. But I wanted the prestige of having a mistress. I chose a girl of rather poor reputation, whose mother had, at some time, I'm not quite sure when, in some way or other, I don't quite know how, been rather rude to the Margravine. The odd thing was that, on the one hand, I didn't love the girl and, on the other, the girl wouldn't let me have her. I'm probably the only man she ever said no to. But the pleasure of making people think, and hearing them say, that I was keeping a mistress was a consolation, both for spending my time with someone whom I didn't love as well as for not going to bed with the woman I was keeping.

The Margravine was greatly offended by my affair; her reproofs only made me feel more attached to the girl. At the same time, the mother of my supposed mistress, who still hated the Margravine and felt flattered by the sort of rivalry that had arisen between the princess and her daughter, kept urging me to do all sorts of things to give offence to the court. In the end, the dowager lost patience and gave orders that I was not to be admitted into her presence. At first I felt very hurt at falling into disgrace and made an attempt to regain the favour that I had done everything I possibly could to lose. I failed to do so and all the people who had hitherto been prevented from speaking openly about my scandalous behaviour were now able to get their own back. There was a general upsurge of criticism and disapproval.

I was so angry and embarrassed that I did further stupid things. In the end, informed by the dowager about all that had been happening, my father ordered me to come and join him in Brussels and we left together for Edinburgh, arriving there on 8th July 1783. My father had old acquaintances there and they welcomed us with the hospitality and eagerness to please and general friendliness for which the Scots are so well known. I was lodged with a professor of medicine who took in boarders.

1783–84

My father stayed in Scotland for only three weeks. When he left, I eagerly got down to my studies; it was the pleasantest year of my whole life. In those days, it was the custom in Edinburgh for young men to work: they formed philosophical and literary clubs. I joined some of them and made a name for myself by my writings and speeches, although I was doing it in a foreign language. I also made a number of close acquaintances, who later on became well known – Mackintosh, who's now a high-court Judge in Bombay, and Laing, who was one of the ablest historians to follow up the work of Robertson, the Principal of Edinburgh University. And there were others.

Among the most promising of these young men was John Wilde, the son of a tobacco merchant. All his friends looked up to him admiringly, despite the fact that most of them came from far wealthier families. He had vast knowledge, worked immensely hard, was a brilliant conversationalist and a man of excellent character. His ability had been recognized when he was made a professor and had published a work which had been very well received.

And then he went completely mad and must now be shut up in a cell, sleeping on a straw mattress – unless he's dead. What a miserable thing the human race is! What hope is there for us?

1784–85

I spent eighteen months in Edinburgh, having a wonderful time. I did a fair amount of work and everybody said nice things about me. But as ill luck would have it, a little Italian, who was giving me music lessons, introduced me to a faro club run by his brother. I gambled, lost and ran up debts left, right and centre, and my stay there was completely spoilt.

When the time in Edinburgh that my father had allotted for me came to an end, I left, promising to pay the people whom I owed the money but leaving them very dissatisfied and with a very bad impression of me. I went back to London where I spent three weeks wasting my time and was back in Paris in May 1785.

My father had made arrangements for all sorts of activities which would have been pleasant had I been willing and able to take advantage of them. I was to be living in the house of Monsieur Suard, where many literary figures used to meet; and he had promised my father to introduce me into the best Parisian society. But as my apartment wasn't ready, I was put into a room in a hotel where I met a very rich and very licentious Englishman whose wild conduct I tried to imitate. Before I'd been a month in Paris, I was up to my eyes in debt. My father was slightly to blame for sending me, an eighteen-year-old, purely on my own trust, to a place where I couldn't fail to make mistake after mistake. However, I did eventually go to live with the Suards and began to live rather more sensibly.

But the mess I'd already got into at the beginning led to consequences that affected me all the time I was in Paris. The final blow came when my father decided he wanted to find someone to keep an eye on me and asked the advice of a Protestant clergyman, who was chaplain to the Dutch ambassador. This minister thought he knew just the right man and recommended someone called Baumier, who'd introduced himself to him as a Protestant being persecuted by his family for religious reasons. This Baumier was a man with no morals, no money and nowhere to live, an adventurer of the worst possible sort. He tried to get me into his power by joining in all the stupid things I wanted to do and he wouldn't have minded seeing me leading the most dissolute and degrading life possible. Quite apart from all his vices, he was unintelligent, very boring and very insolent. I soon got tired of a man who did nothing but go along with me when I visited prostitutes and borrow money from me: we soon quarrelled. I think he wrote to my father and I imagine he exaggerated the unpleasantness of everything he told him about my behaviour, though the bare truth would have been bad enough. My father himself came to Paris, took me back to Brussels and left me there to rejoin his regiment. I stayed in Brussels from August till the end of November, sharing my time living with two families, the d'Ursels and the d'Arambergs, old friends of my father. I was made very welcome there; I also got to know another, less well-known group of Genevans, whose company I came to enjoy much better.

In that group there was a very pleasant-looking young woman, about twenty-six or twenty-eight years old, and highly intelligent. I felt attracted by her, without ever noticing it, until she said something that surprised even more than it delighted me: she let me know that she loved me. I'm writing these words twenty-five years after I first heard her say this, and I still feel grateful for the pleasure I felt.

She was called Madame Johannot and she has a place in my memory different from that of all the other women I've known. My relationship with her was very brief and didn't amount to very much but the gentle feelings she aroused in me were so completely free from any stress or worry that at the age of forty-four I'm still grateful for the happiness she gave me at the age of eighteen.

The poor woman came to a bad end. She was married to an utterly despicable, corrupt and immoral character who, first of all, dragged her to Paris, then joined the ruling party and, despite being a foreigner, was elected to the Convention, which condemned the King to death, and continued to play a cowardly and devious part in it until that all-too-celebrated government came to an end. Her husband later sent her away to a village in Alsace so that he could install his mistress in their house. Then he brought her back to Paris where she was made to live with the mistress and be her servant; his loathsome treatment of her led her to poison herself. At the time, I was myself living in Paris, in her neighbourhood, without knowing that she was so near. She died a few yards away from a man she had loved and who could never hear her name without being moved to the bottom of his heart; and she died, as I say, thinking that she was forgotten and abandoned by every living person.

I'd been enjoying her love for barely a month when my father came to take me back to Switzerland. Before I left, Madame Johannot and I exchanged long, sad, loving letters and she gave me an address which she said I could use to write to her. She didn't reply. I consoled myself but, though I didn't forget her, as you'll see, soon replaced her by other objects of my affection. I saw her again, just once, two years later in Paris, a few years before her troubles began and my feelings for her revived. I went to see her and when I was told that she had left, I was seized by an extraordinary feeling of sadness and violent emotion. It was a kind of dreadful premonition which her sad fate was to justify all too well.

Back in Switzerland, I once more spent a while in the country, studying this and that and occupying myself with a work I'd first thought of in Brussels and which has greatly interested me ever since: a history of polytheism, a subject which, at that time, I didn't know enough about to write four sensible lines. Brought up on the principles of the eighteenth-century *philosophes*, particularly Helvétius, my only thought was to make my contribution to the destruction of what I described as prejudices. I'd been struck by an assertion of Helvétius, the author of

Concerning the Mind, who claims that paganism is far better than Christianity, and I wanted to support that claim (which I'd never studied in any depth or detail) with a few examples chosen haphazardly, and using plenty of epigrams and declamations, which I fancied were original.

If I hadn't been so lazy and carried away by all my wild impressions, I might perhaps, in a couple of years, have produced a very bad book which would have given me a short-lived reputation, which I would have greatly enjoyed. Once my conceit's involved, I've never been prepared to change my views and I'd have been imprisoned in my early paradoxical style for the rest of my life.

1785–86

If indolence has certain disadvantages, it also offers a few benefits. I didn't limit myself to a peaceful studious life for long. Once more love intervened to distract me, and as I was three years older than I was in Erlangen, I committed three times as many idiotic acts. The object of my passion was an English woman of about thirty to thirty-five, wife of the English ambassador in Turin. She had been very beautiful and still had very nice eyes, excellent teeth and a charming smile. She had a very pleasant house and there was a lot of gambling, so I was able to satisfy my taste for that, a taste even stronger than the one I felt for the lady herself.

Mrs Trevor was extremely flirtatious and had that type of sharp and rather affected wit that you often find in that sort of woman – that's the only sort of wit they're capable of. She wasn't on very good terms with her husband, who was away most of the time, and she always had a collection of half a dozen young Englishmen round her. I started frequenting her salon because it was livelier and more distinguished than any others in Lausanne. Then, seeing that most of these young men were courting her, I decided to do the same and wrote her a splendid letter telling her that I'd fallen in love with her. I handed it to her one evening and went back the following day to find out how she'd responded. My uncertainty as to the result of my action had thrown me into such a state of agitation that I was as nervous and excited as if I really was as passionately in love with her as I had up till then been pretending to be. As was appropriate in the circumstances, Mrs Trevor had replied by letter, reminding me of her obligations as a married woman and offering me her great affection and friendship. I should not have paid too much attention to this idea of friendship and gone on to see how far this friendship would extend. Instead, I thought I was being clever by displaying violent despair because she was only offering to be a friend in return for my love. So, when I heard that horrid word "friend" I started flinging myself all over the floor and bashing my head against the wall. The poor woman, probably used to dealing with more discerning people, had no idea what to do in a situation all the more embarrassing because I was giving not the slightest hint as to how she could put a stop to it in a way acceptable to both of us. All the time, I was keeping ten feet away from her and whenever she tried to come any nearer in order to try and calm me down or console me, I moved away, saying that since she could only offer me friendship, the only thing I could do was to die. For the next four hours, that was all she could get out of me. I went away, leaving her, I think, very annoyed at a lover who was making such a fuss over what was, in reality, just a synonym.

I spent three or four months like this; every day I felt more and more in love because every day I found myself facing obstacles I had myself set up, and, what's more, going back to her house as much for my love of gambling as for my love of Mrs Trevor. She showed remarkable patience in putting up with my behaviour, replied to all my letters, continued to see me tête-à-tête and let me stay with her until three in the morning. She got no benefit from it herself and neither did I. I was excessively shy and in an emotional frenzy. I hadn't yet learnt that rather than ask, it's better to take; I was forever asking and never taking. Mrs Trevor must have thought me a very odd sort of lover indeed but as women love everything that proves that they can inspire a great passion, she accepted my behaviour and didn't show me any ill will.

I became very jealous of an Englishman, who couldn't have cared less about Mrs Trevor. I tried to make him fight a duel with me. He thought he could appease me by telling me that far from wanting to poach on my preserves, he didn't even find her very attractive. I then wanted to have a duel with him because he wasn't properly appreciative of the woman I loved. Our pistols had already been loaded when the Englishman, who hadn't the slightest desire

18

to have such a ridiculous contest, managed to get out of it very cleverly by saying that he wanted seconds and he'd have to tell them the reason for our quarrel. When I tried, without success, to argue that he ought to keep the matter a secret, he just laughed and I was forced to give up my brilliant enterprise for fear of compromising the lady in question.

Winter came and my father told me to get ready to go to Paris with him. I fell into dark despair. Mrs Trevor seemed very touched. I'd often hold her in my arms, covering her hands with tears and spent night after night weeping on a bench on which I had seen her sitting. She too wept with me and if I had stopped quarrelling over what was nothing but a matter of words, I should perhaps have completely succeeded in my purpose, but in the end the only result was a chaste kiss from rather faded lips. I finally left in an indescribable state of distress. Mrs Trevor promised to write to me and, as I was taken away, I was so obviously suffering that even two days later one of my cousins, who was travelling with us, tried to persuade my father that I ought to be sent back to Switzerland, as he was convinced I wouldn't be able to stand the journey. But in the end I did stand it and so we arrived. One evening I had a letter from Mrs Trevor, a dull letter, but I was grateful to her for having kept her word. I replied to it in the most passionate terms. I then received a second letter, rather cooler than the first. And in fact, while these letters were going to and fro, I was myself cooling down. I stopped writing and our acquaintance lapsed.

1786–87

However, I did see Madame Trevor three months later in Paris. I felt no emotion whatsoever and any she may have felt was surprise at seeing my complete unconcern. The poor woman still continued to pursue her career as a flirt for a few more years, making herself very ridiculous. She then returned to England and, I was told, went more or less out of her mind and had a nervous breakdown.

My first few months in Paris were most agreeable. I went back to Monsieur Suard and was made very welcome in his circle. I went to dinner at Mademoiselle Clairon's (his mistress) with the Margrave of Anspach and while, at that time, my mind was completely lacking in sound judgement, I could be very amusing and good at producing epigrams, and I knew more than the rising generation of men of letters, though it was all a bit muddled. I was unconventional and people found that amusing. All Madame Suard's women friends made a great fuss of me and the men forgave my impertinence because I was young and it was expressed in words rather than deeds and less noticeable and less offensive. All the same, when I think back at what I used to say and the deliberate scorn I showed for everybody, I still find it difficult to imagine how they were able to put up with me. I remember one day meeting a member of our circle, thirty years older than myself, and, as usual, I started to chat with him, saying how ridiculous all the people were whom we used to see every day. Having made fun of them one after the other, I suddenly caught hold of his hand and said: "I can see I made you laugh about our friends but you mustn't think that because I've been making fun of them with you, I'll treat you any better when I'm talking to them. I warn you that we've not come to any such agreement."

Gambling, which had got me into such trouble already and was going to cause me so much in the future, now brought me into trouble in Paris and wrecked everything that my father's kindness had done to help me.

At Madame Trevor's house in Switzerland, I had met an elderly French woman, Madame de Bourbonne, who was mad on gambling, but a nice woman and something of a character. She'd gamble while driving in her carriage, she'd gamble in bed, she'd gamble in her bath, morning, noon and night, at any time and anywhere she could. I called on her in Paris; every day, she had a gambling party; I immediately joined it and would regularly lose all the money I had on me, which was my father's allowance and everything I was able to borrow, which was fortunately not very much, although I seized every opportunity to run into debt.

In this connection, I had a rather amusing experience with one of the oldest women who came to Madame Suard's house. This was Madame Saurin, the wife of the philosopher, who was the author of the play *Spartacus*. She had been very beautiful, something which she was the only person to remember, for she was sixty-five years old. She had shown herself very friendly towards me and though I rather unkindly made fun of her, I trusted her more than anyone else in Paris. One day at Madame de

Bourbonne's, I'd lost all the money I had, as well as all I could raise by promissory notes. Having difficulties in paying, I thought of turning to Madame Saurin to ask her to lend me what I owed. However, as I myself disapproved of what I was doing, instead of speaking to her directly, I wrote to her, saying that I'd call on her for her reply after dinner. I did so and found her alone. The reason for my visit made me even more shy than usual and as a result I sat for a long time waiting for her to mention my letter. In the end, as she didn't say a word about it, I decided to break the silence and, speaking very emotionally and blushing, I said: "You must be very surprised at what I wrote. I'd be very unhappy if I've given you a bad impression of me by having confessed to you something that I'd never have mentioned if I hadn't felt encouraged by the affection and kindness you've shown me."

I was stumbling over every word, not even daring to look at her. Still she said nothing, so I looked up and saw from her face that she hadn't the faintest idea what I was talking about as I was making my little speech. I asked her if she'd received my letter. She hadn't so I became even more embarrassed and wished I'd kept my mouth shut – providing I could find some other way to solve my financial problems. But I could think of no other way, so I went ahead and started again: "You've been so kind to me and shown such an interest in me that perhaps I took too much for granted, but there are times when a man loses his head. I'd never forgive myself if I've done anything to harm your friendship with me, so I beg you never, never to let me come back to the subject again.

Please don't make me reveal something that slipped out when I didn't know what I was talking about."

"No," she replied. "Why do you doubt my feelings? I want you to tell me everything. So please go on."

She covered her face in her hands; she was trembling like a leaf. And it was then that I realized that she had taken everything I'd said as a declaration of love. This misunderstanding, her emotion and a double bed covered in silk damask standing only two yards away filled me with an unspeakable terror but, like a worm suddenly turning, I fell into a rage and quickly told the reason for my visit.

"I really can't understand why I've been boring you all this time with such a completely trivial matter," I said. "I've been gambling and stupidly lost more than I can afford at the moment, so I wrote to you to ask if you could do me the favour of lending me enough to enable me to clear my debts."

Madame Saurin didn't move. Then she took her hands away from her face, which there was no longer any need to cover. She stood up and, without saying a word, handed me the amount which I asked her for. But we were both so completely at a loss that neither of us spoke. I didn't even open my mouth to thank her.

It was at this time that I got to know the first woman of outstanding intelligence, more than anyone I have ever met. She was Madame de Charrière, a Dutch woman from one of the most distinguished families of Holland. In her youth, she had become notorious for her wit and her strange character. After a number of passionate affairs – some of them rather unhappy – and being already in her thirties, she had, despite the disapproval of her family, married her brother's tutor, an intelligent, considerate and honourable man but the most aloof and phlegmatic you could ever imagine. For the first few years of their marriage, his wife had pestered him a lot, with only brief success, trying to stir him to be as lively as herself; her sad failure had soon destroyed any thought of all the happiness she had promised herself from this in many ways unsuitable match. She had been greatly attracted to a man much younger than herself, extremely good-looking but not very intelligent. I never learnt the full details of this passionate affair but I knew enough from what she and other people told me that she had been very distraught and unhappy and that her domestic life had been very unsettled by her husband's displeasure at her behaviour and that finally, when the young man concerned had left her in order to marry someone else, she had been for a while in a state of utter despair. However, this despair had greatly helped her literary reputation, because it had inspired *Caliste*, one of her more delightful works, which forms part of a novel published under the title *Letters from Lausanne*.

When I first got to know her, this was the book she was busy publishing. I was enthralled by her intelligence. We spent days and nights talking. She judged everybody she knew very severely and I was always delighted to make fun of people. We suited each other perfectly. But we soon found that we had more personal and more important interests in common. Madame de Charrière had such original and lively views on life, such scorn for any sort of prejudice,

such a forceful way of thinking, so vigorous and disdainful a feeling of her superiority over ordinary people, that,
being myself, at the age of twenty, equally inclined to be
disdainful and unconventional, her conversation filled
me with a delight that I had never felt before. I was carried away with joy. Her husband, a very decent man, very
affectionate and who felt beholden to her, had taken her
to Paris to help her recover from having been deserted by
the man she loved. She was twenty-seven years older than
I was, so our relationship gave no reason for him to be
suspicious. He was delighted and gave us every encouragement. I still remember with emotion the days and nights we
spent together, drinking tea and talking with inexhaustible
enthusiasm about every subject under the sun. However,
this new passion of mine still left me time for other things
and, unfortunately, enough to commit a large number of
stupidities and run up lots of debts. A woman who was
in correspondence with my father informed him about
my behaviour, at the same time telling him that I could
remedy the situation by marrying a girl who moved in the
same circles as mine; she was said to have a private income
of some nine thousand francs a year. Naturally, this idea
greatly attracted my father. He told me about it in a letter,
in which he also, quite justifiably, reproached me for doing
a large number of stupid things; he ended by saying that
he was prepared to let me go on living in Paris only if I'd
undertake to try and marry the girl and enquired whether
I had any chance of success.

The girl was sixteen years old and very pretty. Her
mother had been very kind to me when I'd first arrived

in Paris. So I was faced with the alternatives of at least trying to do something, the result of which could have suited me very well, or having to leave a city where I was having a very pleasant time and go back to my father, who strongly disapproved of my conduct. I didn't hesitate: I'd have a go, and began by writing the usual letter to her mother, asking for her daughter's hand. She replied in a very friendly tone but negatively, on the grounds that her daughter was already engaged to a man who was intending to marry her in a few months' time. However, I didn't think that she herself considered that she was giving me a definitive refusal because, on the one hand, as I later learnt, she had made enquiries in Switzerland about my financial situation and, on the other, she gave me every opportunity to talk tête-à-tête with her daughter. And I behaved like a complete idiot. Instead of taking advantage of the mother's good offices – for, despite her refusal, she was being very friendly – I tried to start a romance with her daughter in the most absurd way possible: instead of trying to make her like me, I didn't utter a single word to express my feeling and, when we were alone together, I continued to talk, very shyly, about sheer trivialities. But I then wrote her a grand letter, as if I was writing to someone whose parents were trying to force her to marry a man she didn't love and I suggested we should elope… No doubt she showed my letter to her mother who indulgently allowed her to answer it as if she hadn't been told about it.

Mademoiselle Pourrat – that was her name – replied that it was for her parents to decide what she ought to do and that she didn't like getting letters from a man. I refused to take no for an answer and persisted in my suggestion of eloping, of helping her to be free and protecting her from being forced into a marriage she didn't want. You'd have thought I was writing to a victim who was begging me to help her and who was as passionately in love with me as I thought I was with her, whereas the truth was that my highly chivalrous epistles were being addressed to a very sensible young girl who didn't love me at all and didn't dislike the man whom her parents had suggested as her husband and, what is more, had given me not the slightest right or reason to write to her in such terms. But I'd set out on that course and I was damned if I'd change it.

The most mysterious thing of all in this whole affair was that when I was with Mademoiselle Pourrat I never mentioned these letters. Her mother continued to let me see her alone despite the outlandish suggestions of which she must certainly have been aware. And this confirms my belief that I might still have succeeded. But far from taking advantage of these opportunities, as soon as I was with Mademoiselle Pourrat I was completely overcome by shyness. I talked about nothing but completely insignificant things and didn't make the slightest reference to the letters which I was writing to her every day nor to the feelings I was expressing.

In the end, something happened, through no fault of mine, which finally brought the whole affair to a head: Madame Pourrat had always been fond of men and had a recognized lover. Ever since I had asked her for her daughter's hand, she had continued to be friendly with me, had always seemed to be unaware of the absurd letters I was writing to her daughter every day, suggesting we might elope; I even took her into my confidence as to my feelings and my unhappy state, always, I may say, without a second thought and in all sincerity: I'd decided to follow that course with both of them and I intended to stick to it. As a result, I found myself having long conversations, alone, with Madame Pourrat. Her lover took offence at this and there were violent scenes. Madame Pourrat was nearly fifty and didn't want to lose a lover who might well prove to be her last. She decided that she had to reassure him. I was quite unsuspecting and one day when I was with her, as usual lamenting my fate, Monsieur de Sainte-Croix, the lover in question, suddenly appeared. He was in a very bad temper. Madame Pourrat took my hand, led me up to him and asked me to swear, on my word of honour, that it was her daughter whom I loved and whom I wished to marry and that I had no other reason for calling on her. She considered this declaration she was asking me to make purely a means to put an end to Monsieur de Sainte-Croix's jealous suspicions. I saw the matter very differently: I felt that I was being dragged into the presence of someone I didn't know and, having to confess that I was a forlorn lover, rejected by both the daughter and her mother, I felt so offended in my self-respect that I flew into a frenzy. I happened to have on me a small bottle of opium which I'd been carrying around with me for some time, because, during my relationship with Madame de Charrière, she had been ill and taking a lot of it, which had given me the idea of getting some; and her lively and exuberant but very bizarre talk had thrown me into a state of mental intoxication which had contributed quite considerably to my idiotic conduct at this time.

I kept saying that I wanted to die until I almost succeeded in convincing myself that I really did want to, even though, in fact, I hadn't the slightest desire to. Anyway, having this opium in my pocket and having been summoned to appear before Monsieur de Sainte-Croix, I felt I'd been put into such an embarrassing situation that it was easier to extricate myself by making a scene rather than by having a sensible discussion. I could foresee that Monsieur de Sainte-Croix would be questioning me, weighing me up, and I felt humiliated and couldn't bear the thought of being questioned or assessed or anything likely to prolong the situation. I felt sure that swallowing my opium would provide a diversion. And I'd often had the thought that wanting to kill yourself for the sake of a woman was a good way to impress her – which isn't quite true. When a woman likes you and asks nothing better than to let you take her, it's a good idea to threaten to kill yourself, it provides her with a quick, decisive and respectable pretext. But if she doesn't love you, neither the threat nor actually doing it will have any effect on her. In my adventure with Mademoiselle Pourrat there was one basic mistake: I was the only person participating in the romance. So when Madame Pourrat had finished going through her list of questions, instead of replying to them, I said I was grateful to her for having put me into this situation, which offered me no alternative. I then put my little phial of opium to my lips. I remember that in the very short time it took me to do so, I considered two possibilities, which decided me: if I die as a result, that'll be the end of me, and if someone saves me, Mademoiselle Pourrat can't possibly not be moved by pity for a man ready to kill himself for love of her.

So I swallowed my opium. I don't think there was enough to do me much harm and as Monsieur de Sainte-Croix lunged towards me, I spilt more than half of it on the floor. Everybody was very frightened. They made me drink some acid to counteract the effect of the opium and I meekly did everything they wanted, not that I was afraid but because I would have found it tiresome to argue if they had insisted. When I say I wasn't afraid, it wasn't because I knew the danger was minimal, for I hadn't the slightest idea of the effects of opium and thought they were much more terrible than they actually turned out to be. But after considering the two possible consequences, I'd become completely indifferent as to the outcome. However, my willingness to accept all the remedies they were offering me to counteract the effects of what I'd done must have made the people watching me realize that this tragic behaviour was just a sham.

This isn't the only time in my life that, having done something spectacular, I've suddenly become bored by the thought of the solemn attitude that I'd have to adopt to maintain the effect and, through sheer boredom, deliberately stopped pretending.

After they'd administered all the cures they thought useful, I was given a little sermon, half sympathetic, half reproachful, to which I listened with tragic expression.

Then Mademoiselle Pourrat came into the room – she'd missed all the stupid antics which I'd been performing for her benefit and then proceeded to display my utter inconsistency by tactfully agreeing to help her mother to prevent her from learning what had just happened. Mademoiselle Pourrat was all dressed up to go to the first performance of Beaumarchais's *Tarare*. Madame Pourrat invited me to join them and I accepted. So the tragicomedy of my attempted suicide ended in a night at the opera, which I enjoyed tremendously, either because of the effect of the opium or else – and this seems more likely – because I was so fed up by all this gloom and doom that I needed some relaxation.

Realizing that she must put a stop to my mad behaviour, Madame Pourrat, using my letters as a pretext and claiming that she'd known nothing at all about the whole affair, wrote to me the next day, saying that I had abused her confidence when she was allowing me to continue seeing her daughter while I was trying to persuade her to elope with me. She told me that I would no longer be welcome at her house and in order to remove any hope or possibility of my seeing her daughter, she sent for Monsieur de Charrière and asked him personally to discover from her exactly what her feelings were towards me. Mademoiselle Pourrat told him very frankly that I had never made any mention of love to her, that she had been greatly surprised by my letters, that she had never done or said anything to encourage me to make any such proposals, and that she didn't love me, was very happy to accept her parents' plans for her marriage and fully agreed with her mother's

31

decision to forbid me to call on her. Monsieur de Charrière gave me a detailed account of this interview, adding
that had he seen the slightest sign that the young person
had any liking for me, he would have tried to persuade
her mother to change her opinion of me.

So ended my adventure. I can't say that I felt very sorry.
I had, at times, been rather restive, irritated by all the
obstacles I was meeting and so felt the urge to try to
break them down; there was also my fear of having to
go back to my father. All this had made me persist in this
desperate attempt and my rebellious nature had led me to
adopt the most absurd means, made even more absurd by
my shyness. But I don't think that I had ever really been
in love. One thing is certain: the very next day, I felt no
regrets whatsoever.

Even while I was indulging in all this tomfoolery, there
was really only one person at the centre of my heart and
mind: Madame de Charrière.

During all this period of agitation, my idiotically roman-
tic letters, my idea of eloping, my threat to kill myself, my
dramatic attempt to take poison, I was spending hours,
whole nights, talking to Madame de Charrière, and during these conversations I would forget all my concerns
about my father, my debts, Mademoiselle Pourrat, in
fact, the whole world. I'm convinced that, without these
conversations, I'd have behaved far less wildly. All Madame de Charrière's ideas were based on utter contempt
for all conventions, all customs. We vied with each other
in making fun of everything, we were intoxicated by the
jokes we made about all such things, by our scorn for the

human race. As a result, I came to behave in the same way as I talked, sometimes laughing idiotically just half an hour after doing something with the utmost conviction. The end of all my plans concerning Mademoiselle Pourrat made me feel even closer to Madame de Charrière. She was the only person with whom I could talk freely, because she was the only one who didn't bore me with advice and comment on my behaviour.

As for the other women whose company I kept, some took a friendly interest in me and lectured me whenever they had the chance, others would have liked to undertake the task of educating a young man who had such strong opinions and made their intentions quite plain. Madame Suard decided to find me a wife and had in mind a girl of sixteen, quite intelligent, full of affectations, not pretty and who would be rich, upon the death of her uncle, who was old (and who, incidentally, at the time I'm writing, which is 1811, is still alive). This young person later married Monsieur Pastoret, became notorious for her foolish conduct during the Revolution, had a few affairs, tried to get a divorce, so as to be able to marry a man I knew very well – I'll be talking about him later – and by whom she had a child, did a few wild things in order to achieve her aim and, having failed, artfully decided to adopt a prudish way of life. Today she's one of the most highly regarded women in Paris. At the time Madame Suard was suggesting her to me as a possible wife, she was very keen on finding herself a husband and made no secret of the fact to anybody. But neither Madame Suard's plans, the urgings of a few old women nor the sermonizing of a few others had any effect on me: if I married, I wanted to marry Mademoiselle Pourrat and she was the only girl I liked for her looks. But for intelligence, Madam de Charrière was the only woman I could listen to, look at and really adore. Not that I didn't take advantage of the few hours when I wasn't with her to do other stupid things.

I was introduced by someone to a tart who went under the name of the Comtesse de Linières. She came from Lausanne, a butcher's daughter. A young Englishman had eloped with her by setting fire to the house where she lived and carrying her off to Paris where, after her lover had left her, she had continued exercising a profession which, as she was good-looking, was proving very lucrative. Having succeeded in building up a certain amount of capital, she had got Monsieur de Linières to marry her. Then he'd died and, now a widow and a countess, she had set up a gambling house. She was a good forty-five years old but, not wanting to give up her earlier way of life entirely, she had sent for a younger sister, about twenty years old, with a good figure, tall, lively and as stupid as they come. There were a few decent men who came and lots of crooks. They couldn't wait to swoop on me, in turn. I'd spend half the night there, losing money, then I'd go off to talk to Madame de Charrière, who never went to bed until six o'clock in the morning. I spent half the day sleeping. I don't know if news of my splendid way of life came to my father's ears or whether it was merely news of my failure with Mademoiselle Pourrat which made him decide to remove me from Paris but,

34

at a moment when I was least expecting it, a Monsieur Benay, a lieutenant in my father's regiment, arrived at the Suards' and told me he'd been sent to take me back to my father, in Bois-le-Duc.

I felt rather guilty and the turmoil into which Madame de Charrière had thrown me and the mere thought of everything that I was going to be told was unbearable. Yet I resigned myself and the idea of disobeying my father never entered my head. But our departure was delayed by the difficulty of finding a carriage. My father had left with me in Paris the old one in which we'd come, but with all my financial problems I'd felt that it would be all right to sell it. Monsieur Benay had been relying on it to get to Bois-le-Duc and had come to Paris in a single-seated cabriolet. We tried to get a post-chaise from the saddler who'd bought my carriage but he hadn't got one or in any case, wouldn't let us have one. This delayed us for a whole day, during which time my head continued to be in a turmoil to which my conversations with Madame de Charrière contributed a great deal. While she certainly didn't foresee the effect she would have on me by her constant emphasis on the stupidity of the human race, on the absurdity of its pretensions, and by sharing my admiration of everything odd, extraordinary and eccentric, she aroused in me a strong desire not to keep to the beaten track of normal people. While I didn't have any definite plan of action, for some vague, unknown reason I asked Monsieur de Charrière to lend me thirty louis or so.

The following day, Monsieur Benay came to discuss how we might make our journey and we agreed that, somehow or other, we'd share his single-seater. As he'd never been to Paris before, I suggested we might wait and leave in the evening and he happily agreed. I myself had nothing definite in mind but it would at least delay the dreaded moment of leaving Paris. I had thirty louis in my pocket and I had the rather nice feeling of being in the pleasant position of being able to do what I liked. We went off to dine in the Palais Royal and, as luck would have it, I found myself sitting next to a man whom I'd occasionally met at the house of Madame de Bourbonne and had enjoyed chatting with because he was quite witty. I can still remember his name because this was the last time I met him: 24th June 1787, a day engraved in my memory. He was the Chevalier de la Roche Saint-André, a talented man, a fine chemist, a great gambler and liked by everyone. I started talking to him and, being so concerned about my situation, I took him aside and told him about it very frankly. He probably didn't pay much attention to what I was saying, any more than I'd have done in his place.

In the course of my account, I told him that I sometimes felt like putting an end to all my problems by running away. "And where would you go?" he asked. "England, of course," I replied. "Well, why not go?" he said. "It's a lovely country and the people who live there are very free." "And when I came back," I said, "everything would have been settled." "Certainly," he replied, "with time everything gets settled."

Then Monsieur Benay came up and I went back with him to finish our meal. But my little chat with Monsieur de Saint-André had had two effects: first, I had learnt that other people attached very little importance to a madcap adventure, which, till then, I had seen as something terrible; secondly, that it had made me think of England, which gave me an idea of where to go if I really wanted to get away. That didn't, of course, mean that I had the slightest reason for going to England rather than anywhere else or that I could find there the slightest help for my problems; but it had at least drawn my attention to one specific country rather than any other. However, at first my only feeling was that the time I now had to take a decision was very limited or that indeed it was already too late, for we were intending to leave as soon as we'd finished our meal and Lieutenant Benay would be with me all the time until we left. As we got up from the table, de Roche said to me, laughingly: "So you haven't gone yet?"

His remark made me even more sorry that it was no longer possible to do so. We went back to our lodgings, we packed our bags, the carriage arrived and we got in. I sighed as I realized that this time everything had been decided and as I fingered the thirty louis in my pocket that were now useless, I felt very frustrated.

In the little single-seated cabriolet, we were terribly cramped. I was on the back seat and Lieutenant Benay, who was very tall and, above all, very fat, was sitting on a little chair between my legs, and lurching about with his head jerking to and fro and nearly losing his balance at every jolt. We'd not gone more than ten yards before he started complaining. I complained even more, because I suddenly thought that if we went back to our lodgings I'd have another chance to do what I wanted. In fact, we were still inside the city boundaries when he declared he couldn't possibly go on like that and asked if we could delay our departure until the next day and find some other vehicle. I agreed and took him back to his hotel and reached my lodgings at eleven o'clock that evening. I now had ten or twelve hours to work out what I'd do.

But it didn't take me long to decide to do something mad, far more serious and much more inexcusable than anything I'd done before, though I didn't see it like that. My fear of meeting my father again and all the other sophistries I'd repeated to myself and heard other people repeat about being free and independent had made me incapable of thinking straight. I spent half an hour walking round my room and then, with a shirt and my thirty louis, I went downstairs, asked the concierge to open the door and rushed out into the street. I still didn't know what I was going to do. In general, what had helped me most in making wild decisions, which had at least seemed to suggest I had a very decisive character, had been, in point of fact, a complete inability to take a decision and the feeling that I could always change my mind. So, with the reassurance that I could never feel certain of the consequences of some idiotic action that I might perhaps not take, I'd gradually go ahead, and eventually discover that I had, in fact, taken it.

And this is exactly how I allowed myself to go ahead and carry out my absurd plan to escape. For a few seconds, I thought how I might safely spend the night and asked a woman of somewhat dubious virtue, whom I'd met earlier that winter, if she'd put me up for the night and, with the typical affectionate nature of that sort of woman, she agreed. But I made it clear that it wasn't because I found her so attractive that I wanted to spend the night with her but because I had business some fifty leagues from Paris, and I'd like her to find me a post-chaise as early as possible the next morning. Meanwhile, as I was feeling very confused and wanted to fortify myself, I asked for some champagne, a few glasses of which made me even more incapable of thinking clearly than before, and I spent rather a restless night. When I woke up, I found a saddler prepared to hire me a post-chaise for so much a day, without bothering to ask where I was going but who merely got me to sign an IOU, which I signed with the first name that came into my head, because I had every intention of sending it back when I got to Calais. My kind hostess had also found me some post horses. I paid her the appropriate amount and off I went at a gallop towards England, with twenty-seven louis in my pocket and without having had the time to give the slightest thought to what I was doing.

It took me twenty-two hours to get to Calais. I asked the landlord of the *Hôtel d'Angleterre* to send the post-chaise back to Paris and went off to enquire about packet-boats for England. There was one just about to leave at that very moment. I hadn't got a passport, but in those happier days there were none of those problems which have made things so terribly difficult, as the French, in their efforts to be free, have created a state of slavery for themselves, at home and abroad. I found a man willing to see to all the necessary formalities for six francs, and forty-five minutes after arriving in Calais I was on board and on my way to England.

I arrived in Dover that evening. During the crossing, I'd met a man who was going to drive to London. The following morning I'd reached the immense city, without knowing a single soul, without the slightest idea where to go and with just fifteen louis cash left in my pocket. The first thing I did was to find lodgings, in a house where I'd stayed for a few days on my earlier visit to London. I felt the need to see the face of someone I'd seen before. They didn't have any rooms available but found me one in the neighbourhood. After finding lodgings, the next thing was to write to my father. I told him about my latest escapade and made whatever excuses I could think of. I told him how miserable I'd been in Paris, above all how much I disliked mankind, and produced a few philosophical platitudes about how tiresome it was living in their society and how I wanted to be alone. I asked him to let me spend three months in England, away from everybody and, without realizing how comical I must have sounded, ended up talking about wanting to get married and live quietly with my wife, not too far from him...

The truth was that I didn't really know what to say and what I actually needed was to rest and recover from the six months of moral and physical turmoil I'd been living through, and that finding myself, for the first time, completely alone and completely free, I was longing to enjoy this novel experience. I didn't feel at all concerned at my lack of money and I spent two of the fifteen louis I had left on two dogs and a monkey and took these splendid purchases back to my lodgings. However, I immediately quarrelled with the monkey and when I tried to give him a beating to make him behave, he became so angry that, though he was quite small, I was unable to control him. So I took him back to the pet shop and exchanged him for another dog. But I soon became fed up with my menagerie and sold two of them back for a quarter of what I'd paid for them. My third dog became really fond of me and was my faithful companion in the wandering life I was soon to be leading.

Apart from the worry of not knowing what attitude my father would take towards my behaviour, I found life in London was not unpleasant or expensive. I was paying half a guinea a week for accommodation, about three shillings a day for food and another three for incidental expenses, so I reckoned that my thirteen louis would last me for almost a month. But a couple of days later, the idea came to me of going on a tour round England and I started thinking about how I might provide myself with the means to do it. I remembered the address of my father's banker, who let me have thirty louis. I also found the address of a young man whom I'd got to know in Lausanne and whom I'd been able to help in many ways at the time I was frequenting Madame Trevor's circle. I called on him. He was a very handsome young man and very full of himself, more than any man I've ever known. He'd spend three hours having his hair dressed, holding a mirror in his hand, so that he'd be able to indicate exactly how every single hair should be placed. Nor did he lack intelligence and, like most young Englishmen of his class, had quite a fair knowledge of the classics. He was very wealthy and of very distinguished birth.

His name was Edmund Lascelles and he was an MP, though a rather obscure one. So I called on him. He was very polite but didn't seem to have any recollection of our previous acquaintance. However, since in the course of our conversation he asked me whether he could help me in any way and as I was still thinking of visiting various parts of England, I asked him if he could lend me fifty louis. He told me he was very sorry that he couldn't, on the pretext that his banker was out of town and by various other similar pretexts; he did his best to sound plausible. But he had a Swiss valet, a very decent sort, who knew my family and wrote offering to lend me forty guineas. His letter arrived when I was out of London and I didn't receive it until much later, by which time he'd already disposed of the money. It so happened that in the house next door to mine one of my old Edinburgh friends was living, John Mackay, employed in some rather subordinate position, I don't exactly know what. We were delighted to meet again. I was pleased not to be leading such a completely solitary existence and spent several hours every day with him, though he was far from being very intelligent. But he brought back very pleasant memories and I liked him because we had both been friends of a man I've already mentioned when talking about my stay in Edinburgh, John Wilde, that remarkably talented character whose life came to such an unhappy end. John Mackay gave me the further pleasure of telling me the address of another of the companions I'd met there. This enabled me to spend a few other pleasant evenings but it wasn't any help for the trip I was planning to make. It did, however, give me another reason for going ahead with it, because meeting all these people had revived the very pleasant memories of my stay in Edinburgh. I wrote to John Wilde and received such a friendly reply that I promised myself not to leave England without having seen him.

Meanwhile, I stayed on in London, eating very frugally, with an occasional visit to the theatre and even to whores – spending the money I'd need for my travels, doing nothing, sometimes feeling bored, at others worrying about my father and feeling very guilty but neverthe-less unspeakably happy at being completely free. One day, going round a corner, I ran into another Edinburgh student: he'd become a doctor and was doing rather well in London. He was called Richard Kentish, who's since made a name for himself with a few books that have been quite well-received. We hadn't been very close friends in Edinburgh but had occasionally got drunk together. He seemed most delighted to see me and took me straight away to meet his wife, whom I'd known for a long time because, when I was finishing my studies, he'd come with her to get married at Gretna Green, where you go to be married when the parents don't agree to the union. After marrying her, he'd brought her to meet the people he'd known in Edinburgh.

She was short and skinny, not at all pretty and I suspect rather bossy. She made me welcome. They were going to Brighton the following day and urged me to come with them, assuring me that I'd find many things to do and see there. But it was in the completely opposite direction from the one I wanted to go in and so I refused. But a couple of days later, I thought I might find as much to amuse myself there as anywhere, so I took the stagecoach to Brighton in the company of a turtle that was due to be eaten by the Prince of Wales. On my arrival, I rented a rather unpleasant little bedroom and went to see Kentish in the expectation of having the tremendously amusing time that they had promised me. But he didn't know a soul, had no decent social connections and was spending his time earning some money by treating a few private patients and gaining experience by doing the same in the local hospital. It was all very useful for him but it wasn't at all what I'd been hoping for.

However, I did spend a week or ten days in Brighton because I had no reason to expect anything better anywhere else. This was also discouraging me from undertaking my trip to Edinburgh, though, as you'll learn later, I was mistaken. In the end, while I was growing more and more bored every day, I met a man going back to London and he offered to share the cost, so I suddenly decided one day after dinner to leave with him. I scribbled a farewell note to Kentish and by midnight we were in London. I'd been very scared by the thought of being robbed for I was carrying on me all the money I possessed and wouldn't have known what to do next if I lost it, so I kept a little sword stick handy between my legs, determined to defend myself at all costs and die rather than be made penniless. My travelling companion who probably hadn't got all the money he possessed on him, found my behaviour quite

44

absurd. However, we reached our destination without my having any opportunity to display my courage. Once back in London, I still didn't do anything for several days. Then, to my great surprise, I started to be bored by my independence. Tired of loafing about the streets of this great city where I couldn't find anything interesting and seeing that my resources were dwindling, I ended up hiring some post horses and, first of all, driving to Newmarket. I've no idea why, unless it was the name, which made me think of the horse-racing, betting and gambling I'd heard a lot about: but it wasn't the racing season and there wasn't a soul about but I still spent a couple of days there, trying to think what I could do next.

I sent a very loving letter to my father, promising him that I'd be back soon; I counted up my money (now reduced to sixteen guineas) and, after paying my bill, set off on foot, straight ahead and determined to get to Northampton, near which town there lived a Mr Bridges, whom I'd met in Oxford. On that first day, I walked twenty-eight miles in pouring rain. I was overtaken by night on a road on the deserted and very dismal heaths of Norfolk and once again began to be scared that there'd be thieves about who'd put an end to all my enterprising plans and pilgrimages by taking all my money. Fortunately, I came to a little village called Stoke Ferry, where I received a very cold reception at the inn because I'd arrived on foot. In England only vagrants and the lowest sort of footpads travel like that. They gave me a poor bed, for which I had the greatest difficulty getting clean sheets. Nevertheless, I slept very soundly and next morning, by making a great fuss and putting on airs, I succeeded in convincing them that I was a gentleman – and was charged accordingly.

It was purely a matter of self-esteem, because after breakfast, I walked fourteen miles to King's Lynn, a little shopping town where I stopped for dinner and afterwards stayed on; I was beginning to find this method of travel rather tiresome. The sun had been shining the whole morning overhead and when I arrived I was hot and exhausted. I began by drinking a whole jugful of what they call negus: port mixed with hot water, sugar and spiced lemon, which they had made up at the inn, all ready to serve. I then tried to make arrangements for continuing my journey, but suddenly realized that I was completely drunk, so drunk that I didn't know what I was doing and didn't even understand what was happening. However, I still had enough sense to be very scared at the situation I was in, in a strange town with very little money. It was a very odd feeling to be at the mercy of anyone who might come along. Having no means of responding, defending myself or going anywhere, I locked my door and, knowing that I was safe from any intruder, lay down on the floor and waited until I'd recovered.

I spent five or six hours in this state and the strangeness of my situation, plus the effects of the drink, filled my mind with such vivid and odd visions that I've never forgotten them. I could see myself miles and miles away from home, with no means of support or help, not knowing whether my father had completely rejected me or would ever take me back again, with not enough to live on for a fortnight… and I'd put myself in that situation quite unnecessarily and for no good reason. All the same, despite my intoxicated state, I was still able to think far more reasonably and seriously than I had when I was in full possession of my senses, because then I had made plans and felt capable of action, whereas that drink had taken away all my strength and confused my mind too much to consider making any plans. Then, gradually, my head cleared and I felt sufficiently in control of myself to make enquiries about how I might continue on my travels more comfortably. But my enquiries did little to reassure me. I didn't have enough money to buy an old nag for which they wanted twelve louis, so once more I took a post-chaise (the most expensive method of travelling), for the simple reason that I had hardly any money left. I spent the night in the country town of Wisbech.

On the way, I came across a very fine carriage which had overturned, so I stopped and offered the lady and gentleman who'd been in it a lift in my post-chaise. They accepted and I was delighted by the thought that I wouldn't have to spend a lonely evening, but to my great surprise, when we got out of the carriage, the lady and gentleman bowed to me and went off without saying a word. Next day I learnt that there was a troupe of travelling actors – not very good ones – playing in a barn and since I felt as comfortable there as anywhere else, I decided that I would stay on and go to the show. I can't remember what the play was. Next day, I took another post-chaise and went as far as Thrapston, the closest place to the parish of Wadenhoe, where I was hoping to find Mr Bridges. At the inn, I took a horse and rode straight over to Wadenhoe.

Mr Bridges was indeed the vicar of Wadenhoe but he'd just left and wasn't expected back for three weeks. This information completely upset my plans. Goodbye to any chance of getting any money to go to Scotland… I didn't know anyone in the district and had barely enough money to get back to London and stay there a fortnight, which, in any case wouldn't even be long enough to get a reply from my father. I had to come to a quick decision because every meal and every night's bed was adding to my problems. I made up my mind: I worked out that, by sticking strictly to a plan, I could get to Edinburgh on horseback or by cabriolet on my own and once there I would rely on my friends. Oh, what a wonderful thing it is to be young! Certainly, if I had to travel all that way now and put myself into the hands of people who had no reason to help me, and having no reason myself for behaving as I was, if I had to lay myself open to hearing someone ask me what I thought I was doing, and then be refused what I wanted or needed, nothing on earth could tempt me to try. But at twenty, nothing seemed simpler than to say to my friends: "Look, I've come a long, long way to share your supper, I've not got a penny in my pocket, so you must invite me, treat me kindly, let's all have a drink together, just thank me – and lend me enough money to get back home…"

I felt sure that they'd be delighted to hear me say something like that, so I asked the landlord to come and see me, told him that I wanted to take advantage of my friend Bridges's absence to go and spend a few days at a place some twelve miles away and could he find me a cabriolet.

He brought a man who had one and a very fine horse but unfortunately the cabriolet was at Stamford, a little town some ten miles away. He was perfectly happy to let me hire it and gave me his horse and his son to accompany me to the saddler's where the cabriolet was being repaired; he also agreed that I could go on my trip from Stamford. I was delighted to have solved my problem so easily and the next day I got on the horse, the son of the owner of the horse got on a miserable little nag, which the landlord lent him, and we had no trouble at all in getting to Stamford. But at Stamford there was a problem: they hadn't finished repairing the cabriolet. I tried unsuccessfully to get my companion to let me continue my journey on horseback. He refused, though I thought he might have agreed if, after his first refusal, I hadn't flown into a frenzy of rage and started abusing him. He just laughed at me. I then tried a more gentle approach. He replied that I'd been too rude, got on his nag and rode off, leaving me to my own devices. So my problems were going from bad to worse. I spent the night in Stamford in complete despair.

Next day I decided to go back to Thrapston in the hope of getting my landlord to find me another vehicle. When I again raised the matter with him, he seemed very unwilling to help me. He'd formed a low opinion of me, for a very strange reason that I would never have guessed: ever since my drunken episode with the negus at King's Lynn, I'd been very wary of drinking wine for fear of suffering from the effects and the odd state I'd been in for a few hours. As a result, for the whole time I'd been at the inn at Thrapston, I'd been drinking nothing but water. In England, such abstinence was so unusual that my landlord had found it scandalous, though he hadn't mentioned his bad impression to me himself; I learnt it from the man who'd first lent me the cabriolet and whom I'd asked to come and discuss the matter further. When I complained to him about his son's conduct towards me, he said: "Ah, mister, they're saying very odd things about you." I was very surprised and when I pressed him, he replied: "You haven't touched a drop of wine all the time you've been here."

The penny dropped; but though I immediately ordered a bottle of wine, the harm had been done and it proved impossible to repair the damage; I had no chance of getting a vehicle, so next day I once again hired a horse, pretending I was going to ride over to Wadenhoe to see if Mr Bridges was back yet. As bad luck would have it, of the two horses my landlord had, only the poorer one was available, so, as a result, I got a very small white horse, old and hideously ugly.

I left early the following day and when I'd gone ten or twelve miles I wrote to the landlord, telling him that I'd met a friend who was going to the races at Nottingham and that he'd persuaded me to join him. I had no idea of the risk I was running: English law considered that using a hired horse to go to any destination other than the one stated, was considered theft and all the owner of the horse needed to do was start proceedings against me or put my description in the newspapers. I would certainly have been arrested, put on trial and perhaps sentenced to be transported or, at the very least, taken to court for theft, and even if I was found not guilty, it would have been most unpleasant and, together with my running away to England, would have had disastrous consequences if anyone came to hear of it. In the end, nothing like that happened. The owner of the horse was certainly at first very surprised but then he went over to Wadenhoe where, fortunately, Mr Bridges had returned and, after receiving word from me, vouched that I would come back.

As for myself, I was blissfully unaware of these risks and on that first day did twenty or so miles and spent the night at Kettering, a little Leicestershire village, if I remember rightly. It was then that I really began, for the first time, to taste the joys of being alone and completely independent that I'd been promising myself so often. Up till then, I'd been wandering aimlessly about, unhappy to be doing something which I quite rightly found absurd and pointless. But now I had an aim, not really a very important one, of course, because it was mainly to spend a fortnight with some college friends, but it led me in a definite direction and I could breathe a sigh of relief that it was I alone who'd chosen it.

I've forgotten the various stages of my journey on my miserable little white horse but I do remember that the whole trip was wonderful. The countryside was a delight. I rode through Leicester, Derby, Buxton, Chorley, Kendal and Carlisle, where I crossed into Scotland and came to Edinburgh. I enjoyed the trip too much not to try to recall the slightest details. I was doing thirty to fifty miles a day. For the first couple of days I felt rather intimidated at the inns. My horse was such a pathetic beast that I thought

51

that I looked no richer or more like a gentleman than when I was on foot and I remembered the poor reception I'd had earlier travelling like that. But I quickly discovered the vast difference in attitude to someone on horseback and someone on foot. In England, firms employ commercial travellers who ride all over the country calling on their clients. These travellers live very well and spend a lot of money at inns, so that they're made very welcome. Prices of rooms and dinner are fixed so innkeepers have to compensate themselves by what they charge for wine. Everywhere I went I was taken for a commercial traveller and as a result made very welcome. There were always seven or eight of them to have a chat with and when they discovered that I was a member of the upper classes, they treated me all the better.

England is a country in which, on the one hand, everybody's rights are guaranteed and, on the other, differences of class are most carefully observed. I was travelling for practically nothing: expenses for both myself and my horse didn't come to more than half a guinea a day. The lovely countryside, the pleasant weather, the good condition of the roads, the cleanliness of the inns, the general air of happiness, the sensible and orderly life of the inhabitants are, for any observant traveller, a constant source of enjoyment. I knew the language well enough to be always taken for an Englishman or rather, for a Scot: I'd kept the accent I'd acquired from my first education in Scotland.

I finally arrived in Edinburgh at six o'clock in the evening of 12th August 1787; I'd about nine or ten shillings left in my pocket. I quickly went in search of my friend Wilde and two hours later I was surrounded by all of my old acquaintances who were still in the city at that time of the year. All those rich enough had gone off to their estates. However, there were enough to form quite a large group and they were all delighted to see me. They appreciated the eccentricity of my expedition; things like that always appeal to the English.

The fortnight spent in Edinburgh was one of continuous festivity. My friends all did their best to entertain me and we spent every evening and every night in each other's company. In addition, poor Wilde showed me how fond he was of my company with an openheartedness that really touched me. Who could have foreseen that only seven years later he'd be strapped to a straw mattress! Laing, Mackintosh, Orr, Fleming and Wauchope were all away. And then I had to start thinking of leaving. I had to appeal to Wilde, who managed, with some difficulty but most willingly, to let me have ten guineas. I got on my old nag and left. At Niddrie I'd been to see the Wauchopes, who'd been very friendly to me as a student and I learnt that the elder sister was living in a little town, a spa if I'm not mistaken, called Moffat. Although I couldn't really afford to make a detour, I still wanted to see her, though I've no idea why, because she wasn't a very agreeable sort of person, about thirty to thirty-five years old, ugly, with red hair and a sharp tongue and extraordinarily capricious. But I was myself feeling so cheerful and happy at the welcome I'd received that I didn't want to miss the opportunity of seeing a few more of these nice Scottish people whom I was about to leave for an indefinite period. I never saw them again.

I found Miss Wauchope living on her own, as you would have expected from her character. She appreciated my calling on her and suggested going back to London via Cumberland and Westmoreland. We were accompanied by a poor man whom she'd taken under her wing and we had a very pleasant trip. The benefit for me was seeing a part of England which I would otherwise have missed. I'm so lazy and lacking in curiosity that I never thought of going to see a monument or any particular part of the world or a famous man. I've always stayed wherever I happened to be, until I take a leap which lands me in some quite different sort of place. But I'm never activated by boredom or for fun or for any other of the motives that normally make people want to change their way of life. I have to be gripped by some passion, or an obsession which turns into a passion. This is what makes me seem quite a rational person to people seeing me in the intervals between passions, for I'm perfectly happy with a way of life which isn't at all attractive, yet I'll make no effort to try and find any other way of passing the time.

Westmoreland and the nicest parts of Cumberland – one of them is dreadful – look like a smaller version of Switzerland. There are some quite high mountains, their summits clouded in fog instead of being covered with snow, lakes studded with grassy little islands, lovely trees, pretty hamlets, two or three clean and tidy little towns; add to that complete freedom to come and go wherever you like, with nobody taking the slightest notice of you and without anything at all resembling a police force, considered essential to keep an eye open for possible criminals but whose real aim is to watch the innocent. All this makes travel in England a real joy. In a sort of museum in Kenwick, I saw a copy of the document sentencing Charles I to death, with the signatures of all the judges exactly imitated, and I was very interested to see Cromwell's, who at the beginning of this century had been thought of as a clever, daring usurper but who today is not even thought worth mentioning.

After coming with me, I think as far as Carlisle, Miss Wauchope left me with a last piece of advice: stop behaving so wildly, citing as an example the escapade that had given her the pleasure of meeting me again. I continued on my way with just enough money to get to Mr Bridges, hoping to stock up there with all I would need, enjoying more and more my way of life, in which I remember discovering only one disadvantage: the moment when age might prevent me from riding on horseback. I consoled myself by vowing that I'd go on living like this as long as I could.

Finally, I arrived at Wadenhoe, where I found everything ready to make me welcome. Mr Bridges was still away but returned the next day. He was an amazingly, almost fanatically, devout man but full of affection for me; without my ever having said anything to suggest it, he had persuaded himself that I'd come from Paris especially to see him. He insisted I must stay several days with him and he put my finances back on an even keel. Among the many people he introduced me to I can recall only

Lady Charlotte Wentworth, about seventy years old, for whom I felt a special regard because she was the sister of the Marquis of Rockingham and my political Scottish connections had inspired in me a particular liking for the party whose leader he'd been, the Whigs.

In return for Mr Bridges's great kindness, I was prepared to comply with all his religious practices, though they were somewhat different from mine. Every evening he'd gather a few young men whom he was educating, two or three of his female domestic staff and some peasants employed in his stables or on his estate, read them passages from the Bible, make us all kneel down and then pronounce long and fervent prayers. He'd often literally roll around on the ground, knocking his head on the floor. If there was the slightest interruption during all these exercises, he'd be thrown into despair. All the same, I could willingly have resigned myself to staying on indefinitely with Mr Bridges because I was afraid of going back to my father. But as there was no way I could possibly delay it any further, I fixed the day when I'd leave. I'd given back to its owner my trusty little white horse that had carried me all this way. I was tempted by my fondness for this means of travel to buy another one, not foreseeing the difficulty of getting it out of England. Mr Bridges again vouched for me and once more I set out for London on a far better horse and very pleased to go back to my father in this way. I arrived in London in September, I'm not sure of the exact date, and all my splendid hopes fell to ashes. It had been easy to explain to Mr Bridges why I was short of money but I hadn't told him that I'd face the exact same problem in London; he'd thought that my father's bankers would be able to supply me with the funds and had given me just enough to get to London.

The most sensible thing to do would have been to sell my horse, take a stagecoach and make my way as inconspicuously and cheaply as possible to my ultimate destination. But I'd got to like my way of travelling and so I set about trying to find other ways to do it. I thought of approaching Kentish and called on him; he promised he'd help me to solve my problem and so, on the strength of that promise, I spent my time making the most of what little opportunity I had left of being independent, so soon going to come to an end. I found various ways of spending what money I had left and finally realized that I was penniless. The letters I got from my father during this period also filled me with remorse and this added to my troubles. He expressed his despair at my conduct, at my continued delay to return home and told me that, in order to force me back, he'd told his bankers not to advance me any money at all. I made a final appeal to Kentish, who now changed his tune, refused to show any further interest and told me I shouldn't have got myself into such a situation. I've never forgotten the impression that remark made on me: for the first time in my life, I saw myself at the mercy of someone who was making me realize it. It wasn't that Kentish really intended to abandon me but that, while still ready to help, he didn't disguise the fact that he disapproved of me and that he was doing it out of pity. So his offer to help was really offensive: to avoid giving me any money, he suggested that I could come and dine with him, and in order to make me realize that he wasn't doing this out of friendship but as a kindness to a pauper to whom you offer a meal for four or six days, he said that the most he could offer me was what he and his wife ate, emphasizing that, in his household, meals were organized for two people only.

I put up with this sort of uncivil behaviour because, although my father had forbidden me to contact his bankers, I'd written to them and was hoping to be in a position to tell this so-called friend what I thought of his treatment of me. But as these miserable bankers were, or perhaps were pretending to be, out of town, they delayed answering me for more than a week and when they did it was to give me a firm refusal. So I found myself having a final confrontation with Kentish, to explain my situation. He told me to sell my horse and go wherever I could and wherever I wanted with the proceeds. The only help he had to offer was to take me to a horse-dealer who'd buy it on the spot. I had no other option and after a rather lively exchange, which could have led to a complete end to our relationship had he not shown that he didn't give a damn about either my reproaches or my requests, we went off to see the man he'd mentioned, who offered me four louis for a horse which had cost me fifteen. I flew into a rage, started insulting the horse-dealer, who was in fact only doing his job, and I was in danger of being assaulted by him and his stablemen. Seeing that there was nothing else to be done, Kentish, who was as keen as I was to put an end to the whole affair, offered to lend me ten guineas on condition

I gave him a formal receipt and left my horse with him; he promised to sell it for as much as possible and credit me with the money. Being in no position to refuse, I accepted his offer and left him, vowing never to be so idiotic again.

Still having a weakness for knight-errantry, I wanted to ride hell for leather to Dover, which was not at all the way the English like to travel, because you can go just as fast and more cheaply in a post-chaise. But I would have felt I was demeaning myself if I hadn't got a horse between my knees. My poor dog, which had been my faithful companion throughout all my travels, was the only one to suffer during this final mad act of mine – when I say final, I mean only of those I did in England, which I left the next day. A few miles from Dover, the poor beast became too exhausted to keep up with me, so I entrusted him, half dead, to a postilion, with a letter to Kentish saying that as he treated his friends like dogs, I hoped he'd treat this dog as a friend. Some years later, I learnt that the postilion had done as I'd asked and that Kentish had shown this dog to one of my cousins who was travelling in England, as proof of the close and friendly affection that we'd always had for each other. In 1794, this man Kentish took it into his head to write to me in a similar vein, recalling the delightful times we'd had together in 1787. I replied rather brusquely and since then I've had no further contact with him.

As I was getting off my horse in Dover, a packet boat was just about to leave for Calais. They took me on board and on 1st October, I was back in France. And to date, that's the last time I've seen England, that home of everything noble, of freedom, happiness and wisdom – but where you have to have reservations about relying on the promises of college friends. I'm being ungrateful: I've had a score of good friends and only one bad one.

In Calais, another problem: I calculated that there was no way I could get to Bois-le-Duc to see my father with what was left of my ten guineas. I approached Monsieur Dessin but he knew too much about suggestions like mine from all those tricky customers on their way to or from England to listen to me. In the end, I resorted to a man who was employed at the inn; in return for a watch worth ten louis, he lent me three, still not quite enough to see me all the way home. I then got back on my horse, to ride, night and day, to a destination where I'd be met with disapproval and reproaches.

On arriving at Bruges, I fell into the hands of an old postmaster who, after taking one look at me, was sharp enough to recognize that he could easily make a fool of me. He began by saying that he hadn't got any horses and wouldn't have any for several days, but offered to get me some, at an exorbitant price. I accepted the deal and he then told me that the owner of the horses hadn't a carriage. A new bargain had to be struck or otherwise I'd have to pay for the previous one. I agreed to accept the first offer but when I thought the whole matter had been settled, there wasn't a postilion to drive me. I managed to find one, for an equally excessive fee. I was so overcome by sadness at the thought of my father's despair, which I could see in his last few, heart-rending letters, of what sort of welcome I could expect and of becoming so dependent after having become so used to being independent, that I hadn't the strength to be angry or get into any argument about anything, so I submitted to all the trickery of this miserable postmaster and finally, once again, set off, though fate had decreed that it wasn't going to be a quick journey.

I left Bruges at about half-past ten, so utterly exhausted that I fell asleep almost straightaway. After a fairly long nap I woke up, only to find that we'd stopped and my driver had disappeared. I rubbed my eyes, called out, shouted, swore, and then, just a few yards away, I heard the sound of a violin. It was a tavern where peasants were dancing and my postilion too, dancing like mad.

At the relay before Antwerp, I discovered that, thanks to that foul postmaster who'd cheated me in Bruges, I hadn't enough money to pay for the horses I'd been driving with and, this time, I didn't know anyone. Nor did I know anyone who could speak French and my bad German would be almost unintelligible. I took a letter out of my pocket and tried using sign language to the post-master to explain that it was a letter of credit from a bank in Antwerp. Luckily, as there was no one able to read it, they took my word and I managed to persuade them to let me go on that far, and, still using sign language, I promised that once there, I'd pay them everything that I owed. At Antwerp, I had to borrow from my postilion to pay for the ferry and was driven to an inn where I'd already stayed with my father a number of times. The innkeeper recognized me, paid off my debts and lent me enough to be able to continue on my way. But I'd become so scared

of running short of money that while they were harness-
ing the horses, I dashed round to see a tradesman whom
I'd known in Brussels and got him to let me have a few
more louis, although it was highly unlikely that I'd need
them. Next day, I arrived at Bois-le-Duc. I was in such
an agony of fear that I hadn't the strength to go straight
to my father's lodgings. But I had no choice and so, taking my courage in both hands, I went. As I followed the
guide they'd given me, I was trembling with dread at the
thought of his abuse – and how much I deserved it. His
last letters had been heart-breaking. He'd told me how
bad he'd felt because of my conduct and that if I stayed
away much longer, I'd have his death on my conscience.
I went to his room; he was playing whist with three officers of his regiment.

"So you're back," he said. "How did you get here?"

I told him I'd come, night and day, partly by horse,
partly by carriage. I was expecting him to burst into rage
once we were alone. The officers left.

"You must be tired," he said. "Go and get some sleep."
He went with me as far as my room. I was walking in
front of him and he noticed that my coat was torn.

"I was always afraid what would happen on that trip,"
he said.

He embraced me, wished me a good night and I went
to bed. I was utterly bewildered by the way he'd greeted
me, so much more gently than I'd hoped or feared.

While I was terrified of being treated as I deserved, I
still felt a real need, even if it meant being abused, to have
a frank talk with my father. My disgraceful behaviour

had made me feel more affectionate towards him and I was longing to tell him how sorry I was and discuss my future with him. I wanted to regain his trust and be able to trust him. I was still afraid but hoped it might be possible for both of us to talk more openly with each other.

But the next day his attitude still hadn't changed and during the whole time – two days – I spent at Bois-le-Duc, we had no discussion of any sort and, when I tried to break the icy silence and made an attempt, a rather embarrassed attempt, to tell him how sorry I was, I met with no response. This silence, which I found so distressing for my father's sake, was probably making him suffer just as much for mine. He was probably thinking that it showed a shameful lack of concern for my quite inexcusable conduct and what I was taking for indifference was perhaps hidden resentment. But on this, as on a thousand other occasions in my life, I was victim of my shyness, which I've never been able to overcome; as soon as I could detect no sign of encouragement to continue, the words died on my lips.

My father had arranged for me to leave with a young officer in his regiment who came from Bern, and he confined his remarks to me purely to matters concerning my journey and, when I got into the carriage, I'd not been able to say a word to give him any details about my recent escapade or tell him how much I repented having done it. Nor had he said anything to me to show how disappointed and sad he was.

The officer accompanying me came from an aristocratic family in Bern. My father detested this form of

government and had brought me up in the same principles. At that time, neither my father nor I had realized
that all old governments are gentle, because they are old,
and all new governments are harsh, because they are new.
However, I make an exception for absolute, despotic
forms of government such as Turkey and   ,* because
there everything depends on the will of one single man,
who becomes obsessed with power, in which case the
disadvantages of being new lie not in the institution but
in the man himself.

My father spent his life denouncing the Bernese aris-
tocracy and I followed suit. We failed to realize the very
fact that these denunciations caused us no personal harm
proved that they were unfounded. But they weren't always
harmless. As a result of accusing the oligarchy of being
unjust and tyrannical, whereas they were, in fact, merely
overbearing and guilty of monopolizing power, my father
himself incurred injustice at their hands which, in the end,
made him lose his post, his fortune and the opportunity
to live in peace for the last twenty years of his life.

Sharing as I did his hatred of the Bernese government,
no sooner had I taken my seat in the post-chaise beside
this Bernese officer than I started repeating all the argu-
ments against political privileges, such as depriving people
of their rights, hereditary power, etc. etc., and didn't fail
to inform my companion that, should I ever be given the
chance, I would free the canton of Vaud from the oppres-
sion which his compatriots exercised over it. Eleven years

---

* There is a blank here: Courtney has a note, saying: "Possibly
France." (TRANSLATOR'S NOTE)

later, the opportunity did arise but by then I'd experienced the French Revolution, witnessed what a revolution is like and played a rather futile role to achieve freedom based on justice and so I took good care not to have anything to do with revolutionizing Switzerland. Thinking back on my conversation with that Bernese officer, what strikes me is how little importance people attached at that time to the expression of one's opinions and the particular tolerance that marked that period. If you were to make a quarter of such comments today, you'd never feel safe for a single moment.

When we arrived in Bern, I said goodbye to my companion and took the stagecoach to Neuchâtel and, that very same evening, called on Madame de Charrière. She was overjoyed to see me and we resumed the conversations we'd had in Paris. I stayed there two days and then had the crazy idea of going back to Lausanne on foot. Madame de Charrière thought it was a splendid idea because, she said, it was exactly like my English expedition. From a sensible point of view, that would have been an excellent reason not to undertake a task that might recall that English episode and make me seem like the prodigal son.

So there I was back under my father's roof with no prospect other than of leading a peaceful life. His mistress (at that time I didn't know she was my father's mistress) tried to settle me in as well as she could, which was very well, and my family treated me equally well. But I'd hardly been there a fortnight before my father told me that he'd persuaded the Duke of Brunswick, at that time the commander-in-chief of the Prussian army in Poland, to offer me a position at his court and that I'd better start getting ready to go to Brunswick some time in December. I saw that this might provide me with the opportunity to lead a more independent life than I'd been able to enjoy in Switzerland and I raised no objection. But I didn't want to leave without spending a few more days with Madame de Charrière and I rode over to pay her a visit.

In addition to the dog which I'd been forced to abandon on my way from London to Dover, I'd brought back a little bitch that I'd grown very fond of. I took her along with me. In a wood not far from Yverdon, between Lausanne and Neuchâtel, I lost my way and ended up in a little village, outside the entrance of an old chateau. At that very moment, two men were coming out with a pack of hounds, who flung themselves on my little bitch, not with any intention of hurting her but, on the contrary, of paying homage to her sex. I didn't much appreciate their motives and drove them off with my whip.

One of the two men spoke to me rather brusquely and I replied in kind and asked him his name. He continued to be insulting and informed me that he was the Chevalier Duplessis d'Épendes. After a few minutes of angry exchanges we agreed that I'd call on him the next day and we'd settle the matter with a duel. I went back to Lausanne and informed one of my cousins of what had happened, asking him if he'd come along with me. He said he would but pointed out that by going to my opponent's place myself, I'd seem to be admitting to being the aggressor, that possibly one of his servants or gamekeepers had used his master's name and it would be better to send someone with a letter to Épendes to make sure of the identity of the man I was dealing with and, if it was Épendes, to arrange for our encounter somewhere else. I did as he suggested. The messenger returned with a reply confirming that it was Monsieur Duplessis, a captain in the service of France. The reply was also full of unpleasant insinuations with regard to the fact that I had made these enquiries instead of myself coming to the rendezvous already agreed. Monsieur Duplessis suggested another place, on Neuchâtel territory. My cousin and I set off and on the way there spent all the time laughing and joking. The reason why I make this comment is that my cousin suddenly remarked: "We must admit that we're both going there in an extraordinarily cheerful mood." I couldn't help laughing because he seemed to think he was claiming credit when, in fact, he was merely going to be a spectator. I wasn't claiming any credit for myself either: I don't pretend to be braver than anybody else, but one of my characteristics is to scorn life and even have a secret longing to escape from it, as I'd be avoiding all the unpleasant things that I may still have to face. I'm rather liable to become frightened at the thought of some unexpected nervous shock. But if I'm given a quarter of an hour to think about it, you'll find I'm completely indifferent to danger.

On the way, we found somewhere to spend the night and at nine o'clock the next morning we were at the place as agreed. Here we met Monsieur Duplessis's second, Monsieur Pillichody from Yverdon, also an officer serving in the French army. He was as courteous and elegant as you'd expect from an officer so employed. We had breakfast together, time passed and there was still no sign of Duplessis. We spent the whole day waiting for him in vain. Monsieur Pillichody was furious and could hardly find words to express his frustration and apologies: he'd never forgive him and if he failed to turn up on such an occasion, he'd no longer be a friend of his. "I've been second thousands of times in the past and I've always been the first to arrive on the scene. Unless he's dead, I'll never have anything to do with him; if he dares to ask me to act as his second again, I'll kill him with my own hands."

While he was throwing himself about in despair at such dishonourable conduct, my uncle suddenly arrived, the father of my own second. He'd come to try and protect me from a dangerous situation and was greatly surprised to find me sitting chatting with the second of my opponent who'd failed to appear. After waiting a little longer, we decided to go home. Monsieur Pillichody had gone on ahead and as we were going past Monsieur Duplessis's property, we found his whole family gathered at the side of the main road to express their apologies at Duplessis's conduct.*

Finita la commedia

---

* Those interested in the outcome of this odd affair are informed, in Dr Courtney's edition of *The Red Notebook* (q.v.), that a duel did eventually take place early in 1788, Constant was slightly wounded and both opponents declared that honour had been satisfied. (TRANSLATOR'S NOTE)

ALMA CLASSICS

ALMA CLASSICS aims to publish mainstream and lesser-known European classics in an innovative and striking way, while employing the highest editorial and production standards. By way of a unique approach the range offers much more, both visually and textually, than readers have come to expect from contemporary classics publishing.

∽

To order any of our titles and for up-to-date information about our current and forthcoming publications, please visit our website on:

www.almaclassics.com